The Tale of
Pepper
the
Pony

Terri Wiltshire

ILLUSTRATED BY
Rebecca Archer

Kingfisher Books

NEW YORK

It was the hottest day of the year and all the farm animals were fast asleep in the warm sunshine.

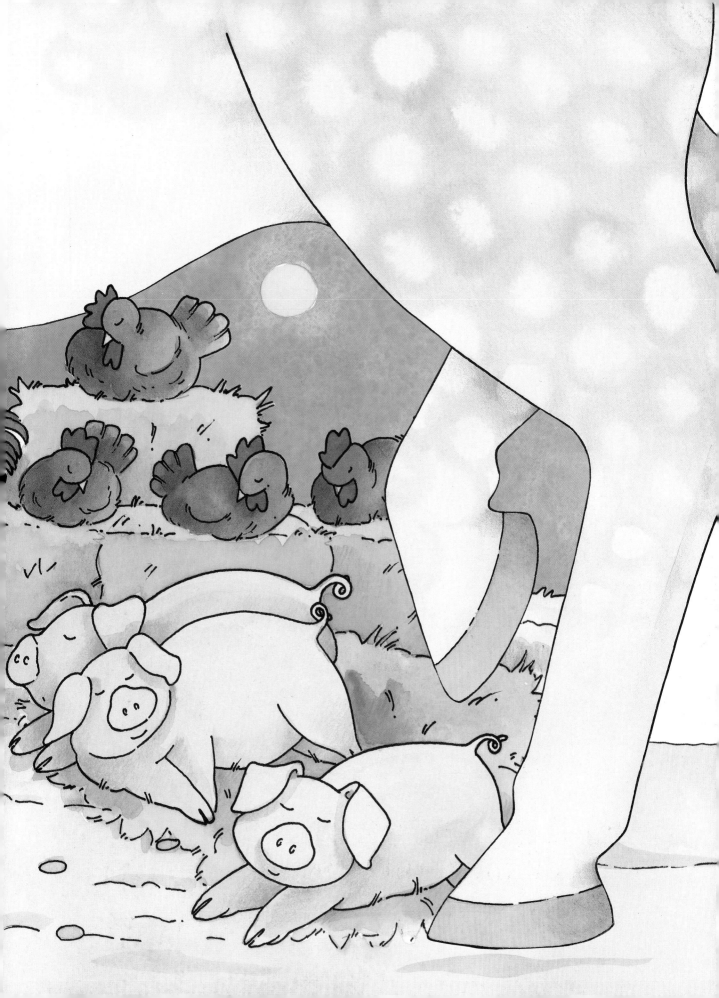

Just then, Pepper the Pony trotted into the farmyard wearing a pretty straw hat trimmed with flowers. None of the animals said anything nice about her hat. They were all too busy snoozing.

Then, suddenly, Pepper stopped and
looked very strange indeed.
Her eyes crossed and her ears fell flat.

Her nose twitched and twisted.
"A-A-A-A-A-A-" went Pepper.
"Look out!" cried the rooster,
waking up.

"A-A-A-chooo!" sneezed Pepper,
so loud that the chickens flapped and
squawked and flew from their nests.
"Bless you," said the roly-poly pig.

"A-A-A-choo!"
sneezed Pepper again,
so loud that the pigs
squealed and
squeaked and sat
SPLAT! in the mud.
"Bless you,"
said the brown cow.

"A-A-A-choo!"
sneezed Pepper once
more, so loud that the
cows' bells jangled
and clanged and rang
in everyone's ears.
"Bless you,"
said the billy goat.

"A-A-A-choo!
A-A-A-choo!
A-A-A-choo!"
sneezed Pepper and, on the last sneeze,
her beautiful flowery hat sailed
across the farmyard and landed
KER-PLOP! by the goats.

"Bless you!"
cried all the animals.
"Delicious!"
said the goats.

"Oh my poor hat," cried Pepper.
"It's ruined — and I've caused
such trouble."

"Never mind, Pepper,"
said the other animals.
"Why don't you come
and join us for a little
...*yawn*...afternoon...
yawn...nap?"
So she did.

KINGFISHER BOOKS
Grisewood & Dempsey Inc.
95 Madison Avenue,
New York, New York 10016

First American edition 1993
2 4 6 8 10 9 7 5 3 1
Copyright text and illustrations © 1993 Cedarwood Press

Library of Congress Cataloging-in-Publication Data
Wiltshire, Terri
The tale of Pepper the Pony/Terri Wiltshire: [illustrated by]
Rebecca Archer — 1st American ed.
p. cm. — (Kingfisher foldouts)
Summary: Pepper the pony parades her hat in front of the other
farm animals, only to lose it when she sneezes. The cover folds out
to provide a backdrop for the story.
1. Toy and movable books — Specimens. [1. Ponies — Fiction.
2. Domestic animals — Fiction. 3. Sneeze — Fiction. 4. Hats —
Fiction. 5. Toy and movable books.]
I. Archer, Rebecca, ill. II. Title. III. Series.
PZ7.W6997Tak 1993
[E] — dc20 92-46249 CIP AC

ISBN 1-85697-858-3
Printed in Hong Kong